W9-CTM-583

Dear Parent:

Congratulations! Your child is taking the first steps on an exciting journey. The destination? Independent reading!

STEP INTO READING® will help your child get there. The program offers five steps to reading success. Each step includes fun stories and colorful art. There are also Step into Reading Sticker Books, Step into Reading Math Readers, Step into Reading Phonics Readers, Step into Reading Write-In Readers, and Step into Reading Phonics Boxed Sets—a complete literacy program with something for every child.

Learning to Read, Step by Step!

Ready to Read   Preschool–Kindergarten
• big type and easy words • rhyme and rhythm • picture clues
For children who know the alphabet and are eager to begin reading.

Reading with Help   Preschool–Grade 1
• basic vocabulary • short sentences • simple stories
For children who recognize familiar words and sound out new words with help.

Reading on Your Own   Grades 1–3
• engaging characters • easy-to-follow plots • popular topics
For children who are ready to read on their own.

Reading Paragraphs   Grades 2–3
• challenging vocabulary • short paragraphs • exciting stories
For newly independent readers who read simple sentences with confidence.

Ready for Chapters   Grades 2–4
• chapters • longer paragraphs • full-color art
For children who want to take the plunge into chapter books but still like colorful pictures.

STEP INTO READING® is designed to give every child a successful reading experience. The grade levels are only guides. Children can progress through the steps at their own speed, developing confidence in their reading, no matter what their grade.

Remember, a lifetime love of reading starts with a single step!

Stephen Hillenburg (signature)

Based on the TV series *SpongeBob SquarePants*® created by Stephen Hillenburg as seen on Nickelodeon®

Visit us on the Web!
StepIntoReading.com
randomhouse.com/kids

Educators and librarians, for a variety of teaching tools, visit us at RHTeachersLibrarians.com

ISBN: 978-0-449-81441-3 (trade) — ISBN: 978-0-375-97162-4 (lib. bdg.)
Printed in the United States of America *5155 7337 4/13*

10 9 8 7 6 5 4 3 2 1
Random House Children's Books supports the First Amendment and celebrates the right to read.

STEP INTO READING®

STEP 2

nickelodeon

SpongeBob SquarePants

The Great Train Mystery

Adapted by David Lewman

Illustrated by The Artifact Group

Based on the screenplay "Krabby Patty No More" by Casey Alexander, Zeus Cervas, Steven Banks, and Dani Michaeli

Random House 🏠 New York

Mr. Krabs needs a recipe.

It is in a locked box.

Mr. Krabs gives

SpongeBob

the key to the box.

SpongeBob and Patrick
will get the recipe.
They take a train.

Plankton is
on the train.
He wants the key.

SpongeBob and Patrick
are very hungry.
They go to the dining car.

SpongeBob and Patrick
meet a nanny
and her baby.

SpongeBob meets
a porter.

The porter does not like
SpongeBob.

He pushes SpongeBob

off his seat!

SpongeBob and Patrick
leave the dining car.
They want to hide
the key.

The key is gone!
SpongeBob cannot
find it!

SpongeBob sees
Plankton.
He thinks Plankton
stole the key!

Patrick checks Plankton.
Plankton does not have
the key.

Patrick lets Plankton go.
SpongeBob asks Patrick
to call the cops.

Patrick shouts

for the cops.

The cops arrive.
SpongeBob tells them
about the missing key.

SpongeBob points
to the baby.

"The baby has the key,"
SpongeBob says.

SpongeBob points
to the nanny.
"She stole the key!"
he says.

SpongeBob holds
the baby.
The police chief
searches the baby.

He finds a stolen jewel!

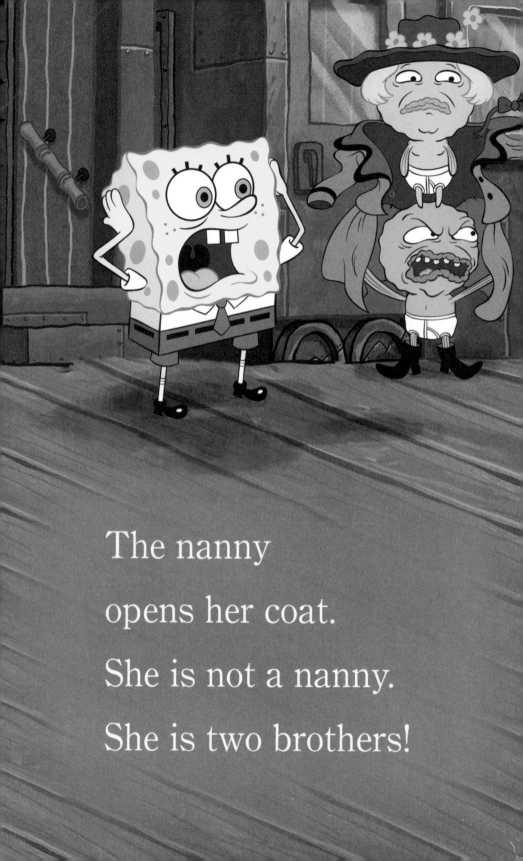

The nanny
opens her coat.
She is not a nanny.
She is two brothers!

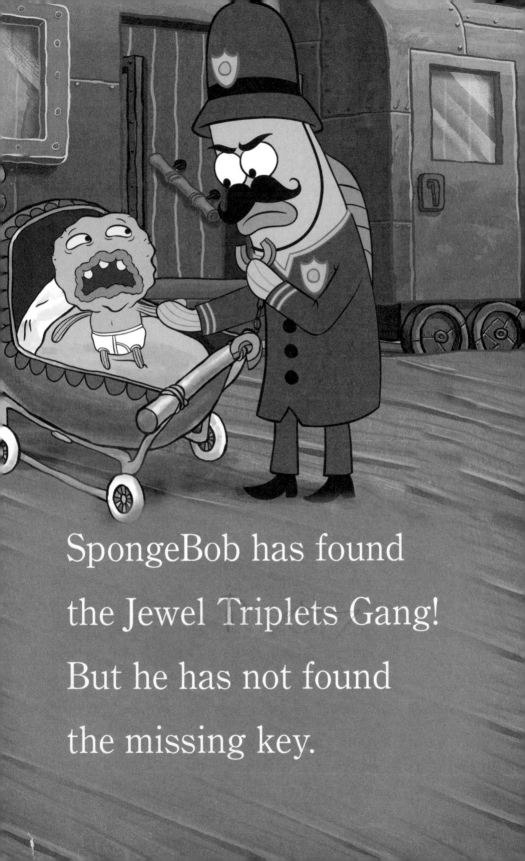

SpongeBob has found
the Jewel Triplets Gang!
But he has not found
the missing key.

SpongeBob thinks
the porter stole the key.
Plankton wants the key.
He jumps on the porter.

A policeman shakes
the porter.
A stapler, a hammer,
and an anvil fall out!

A mask falls
off the porter.

He is really
a ham sandwich thief!
But SpongeBob still
has not found the key.

Wait!

Patrick has something.

It is the key!

He gives SpongeBob
the key.

SpongeBob and Patrick
solve the mystery!
Now they can get
the recipe.
Plankton is
right behind them.